The Stray

ALSO BY DICK KING-SMITH

Babe: The Gallant Pig
Harry's Mad
Martin's Mice
Ace: The Very Important Pig
The Toby Man
Paddy's Pot of Gold
Pretty Polly
The Invisible Dog
Three Terrible Trins
Harriet's Hare

DICK KING-SMITH

The Stray

ILLUSTRATED BY WAYNE PARMENTER

CROWN PUBLISHERS, INC., NEW YORK

Published by Crown Publishers, Inc., a Random House company, 201 East 50th Street, New York, New York 10022

CROWN is a trademark of Crown Publishers, Inc.

http://www.randomhouse.com/

Printed in the United States of America

Library of Congress Cataloging-in-Publication Data
King-Smith, Dick.
The stray / by Dick King-Smith ; illustrated by Wayne Parmenter. — 1st ed.
p. cm.

Summary: When seventy-five-year-old Henny Hickathrift runs away from the old people's home, she meets five children and their parents who welcome her into their family.
[1. Old age—Fiction. 2. Runaways—Fiction. 3. Family life—Fiction.]
I. Parmenter, Wayne, ill. II. Title.

PZ7.K5893St	1996
[Fic]—dc20	96-4230

ISBN 0-517-70934-1 (trade)
0-517-70935-X (lib. bdg.)

10 9 8 7 6 5 4 3 2

First Edition

1
Escaping

Early one morning Henny Hickathrift woke with her mind made up. That very day she would run away from home.

To be more accurate, she would run away from the Home—the old age home where she lived.

I'm bored, she said to herself. I'm bored with this boring place and all the boring old people who live in it, and I'm not staying here a moment longer.

So she got dressed, packed up her very few possessions in a little suitcase, and wrote a note, which she left on her pillow.

It said:

GONE TO STAY WITH MY SISTER IN BIRMINGHAM.

—HENRIETTA HICKATHRIFT

Not only did Henny have no sister in Birmingham, she had no sister at all—or brother, or other living relatives. Her mother and father had died ages ago, for Henny was seventy-five years old.

Now, suitcase in one hand, cane in the other, she sneaked out of the old age home, making sure that no one saw her leave, and set off down the road.

It was a lovely sunny summer's morning, just right for running away, and Henny was so much enjoying her newfound freedom that she walked happily along without really thinking where she was going.

But after a while the suitcase began to feel rather heavy and her feet a bit sore, so she sat down on a park bench for a little rest. Nearby, some children were playing with a soccer ball, which presently rolled across the path and hit Henny Hickathrift quite gently on the legs.

A boy came running up.

"Sorry," he said. "You all right?"

"Fine, thanks," said Henny. "I'm running away from home."

"Oh," said the boy. "Where are you going to?"

Where am I going? thought Henny. I know!

"To the seaside," she said.

"Oh," said the boy. "That will be nice." And he picked up the ball and ran off.

"It will," said Henny. "I haven't been to the seaside since I was a girl, and the weather's lovely, and I've still got quite a bit of this month's pension money left, so why don't I go by train? I haven't been on a train in ages either."

Off she set again, and found her way to the train station. There, the first thing she saw was a big colored poster stuck on the wall. It showed a picture of a happy family on the beach, the mother and father relaxing in deck chairs, watching the children building a big sandcastle. The sands were golden, and in the brilliantly blue sky flew snow-white gulls.

COME TO SUNNY SALTMOUTH! it said.

"I will," said Henny.

She went to the ticket office.

"A single ticket to Saltmouth, please," she said. "Third class."

The ticket clerk peered out of his window. He

saw a little old lady wearing an overcoat that had seen better days and a woolen hat like a tea cozy on top of her short gray hair.

"There's no such thing as third class nowadays," he said with a sniff. "It's either first or standard class."

"Oh," said Henny. "How much is it?"

"Do you have a senior citizen's pass?"

"No."

"In that case, a standard class single ticket to Saltmouth is £32.50."

"That's a lot of money," said Henny.

"It's a long way," the clerk said shortly. He drummed on the window ledge with his fingertips, eager to be rid of this customer, and looked over her head as though she were delaying a long line of people, though in fact no one was behind her.

How rude he is, thought Henny. In the old days he'd have called me madam, with a smile perhaps, and anyway, I don't like people who can't look you in the eye.

She took out her purse. There was £50 in it.

"How much is it, first class?" she asked.

"First class?" said the clerk in a voice that seemed to express amazement that such a person could even contemplate traveling thus.

"Yes. That's what I asked."

"Forty-five pounds."

Henrietta Hickathrift remembered a favorite saying of her mother's. Might as well be hung for a sheep as a lamb, she thought, and she drew herself up to her full height of five feet and one inch and said, "Kindly give me a first class ticket."

The train for Saltmouth was not due for half an hour, so Henny went into the station café and bought herself a cup of coffee (which cost her a pound of the five she had left). Then she sat and waited with excitement for the train to come puffing into the station. But when it arrived, it didn't puff at all. It hummed. There was no hiss of steam, no plume of smoke coming from the funnel of the locomotive, no funnel at all.

Henny clambered aboard and found herself a seat in the first class compartment. How different it was from the last time she had traveled by train! There was no corridor in the long open carriage, just a door at each end that opened in front of you as if by magic, and the windows were huge, and the seats so comfy, and my, how fast they were going!

Henny sat with her cane and her suitcase beside her—the compartment was almost empty—and watched the countryside flashing past at a tremendous speed. She thought of all the old people at the Home, slumped in their chairs watching TV and arguing about which channel they should have on.

Poor old things, she said to herself. I can't think how I put up with it so long. And because she felt so happy to be out of the place, and so comfortable in these first class surroundings, and a bit tired, she shut her eyes and went to sleep.

She was awakened by a deep voice.

"Tickets, please," it said.

The ticket collector was a large man who looked her, she was glad to see, straight in the eye and smiled, showing a lot of very white teeth, and said in a voice like warm honey, "Sorry to wake you, ma'am."

Henny smiled back and handed him her ticket.

"I'm running away from home," she said. "I'm going to the seaside."

"Glad to hear it, ma'am," said the ticket collector. "You'll get nice and brown, this weather." And he went on his way.

After he had gone, Henny suddenly realized that she was very hungry. She had heard an announcement saying that there was a café car in the rear of the first class compartment. Now she thought, It's ten o'clock and I haven't had any breakfast.

She went along and stood in front of the counter and looked at all the different sorts of food and drink that were for sale. She thought of the usual boring breakfast that the old people at the Home would have had and decided she would have things she really liked. "In for a penny, in for a pound" was another of her mother's sayings, and Henny still had four pound coins left.

"I'll have one of those Danish pastries, please," she said, "and a prawn and mayonnaise sandwich and a Mars bar."

"Anything to drink?" asked the steward. "Tea? Coffee?"

"I think I'll have a Coca-Cola," said Henny. "I've never tried one of those before. Oh, and I'd better have a box of jujubes."

The steward looked curiously at this little old lady with the tea cozy hat who had ordered such a strange breakfast.

"You see, I'm going to the seaside," said Henny. "I'm running away from home."

The steward raised his eyebrows.

"Fancy!" he said. "That'll be £3.99 altogether, please."

After she had finished—and much enjoyed—her meal, Henny settled back in her comfortable first class seat and went to sleep again. So soundly did she sleep that when she woke, it was to find that it was midday and that the train had arrived at Saltmouth.

Cane in hand, carrying her little suitcase, Henrietta Hickathrift made her way out of the station and set off along a road that was signposted TO THE BEACH. In the pocket of her old overcoat was her purse, and in the purse was her total worldly wealth—one penny.

She spent all that afternoon on the Saltmouth

sands. They were just as golden as they had been in the poster, and the sky as blue and the gulls as white, and there were children building sandcastles and moms and dads relaxing in deck chairs. Henny couldn't afford one of those, so she sat on her suitcase instead and watched the waves breaking and the sun glinting on the water and ate several of her jujubes and was perfectly happy. Not until much later did she begin to think about what to do next.

She looked around and saw that the beach was almost empty. The families had all gone back to their hotels or their bed-and-breakfasts for dinner. Only a few people were still walking along the sands, and the sea was much closer to her now, for the tide was coming in.

Near to her, a solitary, thin mongrel dog was nosing about, searching for scraps of food. It wore no collar and did not seem to belong to anyone. It's a stray, Henny thought, that has no home. Like me. I've run away from mine. She popped the last of the jujubes into her mouth, and then she picked up her cane, smiling to herself. With the point of it she wrote on the sand in large letters:

Then she picked up her suitcase, made her way up the beach, and climbed the long flight of steps that led to the esplanade high above. At the top she stopped to rest, leaning against the iron railing that flanked the road and looking down to the sands below.

The beach was empty now. Even the dog had gone, and all that remained to be seen was her message, toward which the tide was now creeping. As Henny waited to see her words washed out, she heard voices close by.

"Look!" said one.

"What is it?" said another.

"Where?" said other voices.

"There," said the first voice.

Near Henny, five children stood at the railing. They were all of different sizes, ranging from a tall girl to a small boy, but they all had red hair, and they all were gazing down at the message far below.

"What does it say?" asked the smallest, and the tallest read it to him.

Then they all watched in silence until the waves reached the writing and drowned it.

"How sad," said the tall girl quietly. "I wonder who wrote that."

"I did, actually," said Henny.

The five red-haired children turned and stared at her in solemn silence.

"I had better introduce myself," she said. "My name is Henrietta Hickathrift."

"We are called Good," said the tall girl. "I am Angela, and these are my sisters Eleanor and Rosie and my brothers Barney and Rowley."

"And you're all here for your vacation?" said Henny.

"No," said Angela. "We live in the town."

"Rowley Good, Ivy Cottage, St. Edmund's Street, Saltmouth," chanted the smallest, as he had been taught to do in case he got lost.

Then he said, "And where do you live?"

"Well, nowhere, actually," said Henny. "You see, I've run away from home."

"Why? Were you unhappy?" asked Rowley.

"Yes."

"Well, where are you going to sleep tonight?" asked Angela.

"I don't know."

"I do," said Angela. "Barney, take Miss Hickathrift's suitcase. Eleanor, Rosie, hold Rowley's hands while we cross the road." Then, turning to Henny, she said, "Would you like to follow us?"

A friend in need is a friend indeed, as Mother would have said, thought Henny, let alone five friends. And she did as she was asked.

Five minutes later the procession arrived outside a long low white house that overlooked the harbor with its rows of moored boats, and Angela knocked on the front door.

As it opened she said, "Mom, we've brought a lady home with us."

"She's got nowhere to sleep tonight, Mom," said Barney and Eleanor and Rosie.

"She's a stray," said Rowley.

2

ARRIVING

Ivy Cottage was one of the oldest houses in the seaside resort of Saltmouth. Long ago, when the town had been no more than a fishing village, it had been three cottages—fishermen's homes—but they had since been made into one. And now, because it was long and low and white-washed and had its own small lawn that ran down in front of it to the sea wall, it looked like a country home—in contrast to the tall Victorian buildings that stood behind and to either side of it.

Henny Hickathrift didn't notice any of this at the time, of course. Partly she was a bit tired after her long journey, partly a little dazed from sitting in the sun, but mostly she felt herself to be in a dreamlike state, happy to follow these red-haired children wherever they wanted to go.

14

Now she saw, in the doorway of Ivy Cottage, a tall fair-haired woman, and said, as she often did, the first thing that came into her head.

"They don't get it from you, then?"

Mrs. Good smiled, looking, Henny was glad to see, very directly at her, and said, "The hair, you mean?"

"Yes."

"No, that comes from my husband's side of the family."

"Is he red-haired?"

"Well, more gray now, what's left of it."

"My mother," said Henny, "used to tell me that red-haired men were bad-tempered."

The children's mother laughed.

"Not this one," she said. "He's pretty even-tempered. But do come in"—she paused and glanced at Henny's left hand and saw no rings—"Miss . . ." She paused again.

"Hickathrift," said Henny. "Henrietta Hickathrift."

"I'm Mary Good. Do come in, and Angela, would you put the kettle on? I'm sure Miss Hickathrift would like a cup of tea."

15

"Please call me Henny. Everybody does," said Henny.

"Can we call you Henny?" asked Rowley.

"I don't think—" began his mother.

"Of course you can," said Henny. "Because I'll tell you a secret. I'm one of those funny people that actually like children."

"How many children have you got?" asked Rowley.

"I'm sorry," said Mary Good quickly. "He's only four, and . . ."

"No, don't worry," said Henny. And to Rowley she said, "I never had any children, worse luck. You see, I never married. A long time ago, during the Second World War, I was engaged to be married to a soldier, but he was killed, and after that I never wanted to marry anyone else."

Angela, who had come in with the tea things in time to hear this, looked sad, as did Eleanor and Rosie.

Barney looked interested, for he was working on a school project on the Second World War and wanted to ask questions about this long-dead soldier—what regiment was he in? what was his

16

rank? in what battle did he die?—but didn't think he should.

Rowley only said, "Can I have a cookie?"

"Funny to think," Henny said to the children, "that if I had had a daughter, she'd have been about the same age as your mom, I imagine." To Mary Good she said, "Tell me how old all these people are."

"Well, like I said, Rowley's four, nearly five, and Rosie is seven, and Eleanor's nine, and Barney is eleven, and Angela is thirteen. Milk? Sugar?"

"Both, please," said Henny.

"Will you have a cookie?" asked Angela. With the tea things was a plate of cookies—the kind filled with squashed raisins.

"Ooh!" said Henny. "We used to call those squashed flies when I was young. I've always loved them."

"How old are you now?" asked Rowley.

"Rowley!" said everyone, but Henny only smiled at him and said, "As old as my tongue and a little older than my teeth."

"Dad knows all about them," said Rowley.

"He's a dentist, Dad is. Can I have another cookie, Mom?"

"He's had three already!" said several voices, and Rowley's mother said, "No, you can't."

Henny said, "Actually, if you really want to know, Rowley, I'm seventy-five years old. Today."

"Today?" cried everyone. "It's your birthday?"

"Yes. I woke up early this morning and I thought—Well, old girl, no one's going to give you a birthday present, so you might as well give yourself one. So I did. I ran away. That was my present to myself."

"Because you were unhappy, Henny," said Angela. "That's what you told us."

"Yes. You see, I've been living in an old age home, and I don't really feel like an old person, and it certainly didn't feel like home. Mind you, I did think of a couple of things my mother used to say. One was 'Look before you leap,' and another was 'There's no fool like an old fool.' But then yet another one was 'There's no time like the present.' So I scampered."

"And now you've burned your bridges," said Mary Good.

"Yes, just what Mother would have said. And now I really must be going. Thank you for the tea and the squashed flies. You've been very kind."

"Just a moment," said Mary Good. "I understood the children to say that you had nowhere to sleep tonight?"

"I expect I'll find somewhere," said Henny.

"You already have."

Henny looked at Mary Good and saw that she was smiling. People smile for different reasons and in different ways. This, Henny thought, was an especially nice smile, warm and welcoming.

"Are you offering me a bed for the night?" she asked.

"I am."

"It's very kind of you, Mrs. Good . . ."

"Mary."

"Mary. But the fact is, I couldn't possibly afford it," said Henny. "You see, I've used up all my money running away. To tell you the truth, all I've got left is one penny."

"Listen, Henny," said Mary Good. "We all heard you say just now that no one was going to give you a birthday present. Well, you were wrong. We're going to give you one. We'll find you somewhere to sleep tonight. I'll tell you what, children—let's give Henny a birthday feast to celebrate."

"Can we help with it?" asked Angela, Barney, Eleanor, and Rosie.

"Can we have ice cream?" asked Rowley.

When the children's father arrived home from his dental office and walked into the sitting room of Ivy Cottage, neither his wife nor any of his five children were there (since they all were busy in the kitchen). Instead he saw a little old lady sitting in one of the armchairs.

"Hello!" he said. "Where have you sprung from?"

"From an old age home, actually," said Henny. "I ran away." She looked up at this large man. What hair he had left was reddish, she saw, tinged with gray.

"So you're not bad-tempered," she said.

The dentist shook his head in bewilderment.

"No," he said.

At this point Rowley came in carrying a bowl that he was scraping out with a spoon.

"They made the pudding in this," he said. "D'you want a lick, Henny?"

Taking advantage of this diversion, Rowley's father dodged out of the room and went in search of his wife.

"Mary," he said. "What on earth is happening? There's a strange old woman in the sitting room talking a lot of nonsense. Is she crazy?"

"No, George, not in the slightest," said his wife.

"She's called Henrietta Hickathrift, Dad," said Angela, "and we're giving her a birthday party."

"And she was going to marry a soldier," said Barney, "but he got killed."

"And she's only got one penny in the world," said Eleanor.

"And," said Rosie, "she likes squashed flies."

"It must be me that's gone mad," said George Good. "I think I need a drink."

"Ask Henny what she'd like," said his wife.

Going back to the sitting room, he found Rowley deep in conversation with the old lady.

"Can you swim, Henny?" Rowley was asking.

"Yes. Though I haven't for ages."

"I can, with water wings. I'm going to be an

Olympic swimmer, probably, and win a gold medal, I expect."

"Um, Miss, um, Hickathrift," said George Good. "May I offer you something to drink?"

"Call her Henny, Dad," said Rowley. "Everyone does."

"Do you have any Coca-Cola?" said Henny.

"Can I have some, Dad?" said Rowley.

"Nothing stronger?" his father said to Henny.

"Oh, no, thank you. I had Coca-Cola for my breakfast, and I thought it very strong. In fact, it sent me straight to sleep. It's a good thing that nice ticket collector came along before breakfast—he'd have had a job to wake me, I daresay. You'd have been interested in his teeth. White as snow."

"Really?" said the dentist. "I think I'll have a little whisky." And he poured himself a large glassful.

"Rowley," he said. "Run to the kitchen and see what Mom would like and if the others want Coke too." Then he handed Henny her glass and raised his own.

"Well, cheers!" he said.

Henny did not recall her late father's sayings in the way that she remembered her mother's, perhaps because he had been a man who never said much. But it came to her at that moment what he always said when he had a drink.

"Here's mud in your eye!" she replied.

George Good took a large gulp of whisky.

"Your first visit to Saltmouth?" he asked.

"Yes."

"And where are you staying?"

"Here," said Henny.

3

STAYING

Raiding her freezer, Mary Good had put together a feast. There was even a cake with H. H. on it in silver decorations, and seven and a half candles (one for each ten years and a half candle for the extra five), and everyone sang "Happy birthday, dear Henny, happy birthday to you"—the children very loudly, as though they had known her all their lives.

Ivy Cottage—because it had originally been three dwellings—had a good number of bedrooms. Not till the children were all in theirs and the stray had also gone to bed did George Good have a chance to speak to his wife about their surprise visitor.

"Look, Mary," he said, "I quite see that you couldn't turn the old girl away, but presumably she will find somewhere to go tomorrow? I mean,

she's quite a character, I can see that, and the children seem almost to have adopted her already—it's been Henny this and Henny that all night long—but if we're not careful, we shall have a job getting her out, now that she's got her feet under the table. You'll be saying 'Just for one more night, just for a week' and so on. I know you, you're too softhearted."

"All right, George," said Mary Good. "We'll let her have a good night's sleep, and then tomorrow you can throw her out."

"Throw her out? Me?"

"Yes. I'm not going to. Not yet, anyway."

One of the spare bedrooms at Ivy Cottage was part of an extension that had been built on to the end. The lower part was a double garage, and above was one small bedroom with its own little bathroom. A flight of outside wooden stairs with a handrail led up to it. The family called it the apartment.

The next morning Angela climbed these stairs with a cup of tea and knocked on the bedroom door. There was no answer, even when she knocked again—loudly—and called "Henny!"

27

Awful thoughts ran through Angela's mind. Had yesterday been too much for the runaway at her age? Was her birthday to be followed by her dying?

She peeked in. The room was empty. But then she saw that the little suitcase was still there, as well as the tea cozy hat. But no cane.

Angela dashed down the stairs and ran across the lawn to look over the sea wall. In the harbor below, a few boatmen were messing around, doing whatever it is that people do to their boats. Then Angela saw, on the sands beyond, a small gray-haired figure trudging along.

"Henny!" shouted Angela, waving, and the figure waved back with her cane.

"Where have you been?" said Angela when they met.

"For a nice walk," said Henny. "The seagulls woke me up, sitting on the roof above, cackling, and I looked out and saw what a lovely morning it was, so off I went. Did you think I'd run away again?"

Angela didn't say what she had thought. Instead she said, "You won't, will you?"

"Well, I'll have to go somewhere," said Henny. "Why?"

"Because your mom and dad don't want to be saddled with a penniless stranger."

"You're not a stranger," said Angela. "I feel as if I've known you for a very long time. And you're not penniless—you've got one left—and anyway, I've got some money saved that you can have, and we were talking yesterday evening and the others all said they'd give you some of their pocket money. Except Rowley. He said he couldn't afford to give any of his, but he'd lend you fifty pence."

"You're all very kind," said Henny. "Good by name, good by nature."

After breakfast George Good rose from the table, saying, "Have a lovely day, then, everyone. You're lucky, you are, all on vacation in this lovely weather, while I'm stuck indoors, peering into people's mouths."

"George," said his wife. "Didn't you have something to say to Henny?"

"To Henny? Oh. No, no, I don't think so."

"Adieu, perhaps?"

"Adieu? No, no, it seems that it would be more correct to say *'Au revoir,'*" said the dentist, and suppressing a sigh, he set off to walk to his office.

"Was that French?" asked Rowley.

"Yes," said the others.

"I know some French," he said.

"What?"

"Bong jooer."

"Bong jooer," they all replied.

"Can you clear the table, children," their mother said, "and do the dishes between you? I want to have a quiet chat with Henny."

"Can I have a quiet chat too?" asked Rowley.

"No."

"Okay," said Rowley. "Oh rev-wah."

Once they were sitting comfortably in armchairs, Mary Good said, "Now tell me, what are your plans? I mean, have you thought better of this running away business? Wouldn't it be more sensible to treat it all as just an outing and go back to your old age home? We'd pay for your train fare—you don't need to worry about that. It's not that I imagine it's much fun living in a place like that, but presumably they look after you quite well, and then there's your pension money. They must have that. Shouldn't you go back?"

"Never," said Henny.

"What will you do, then?"

"Well, Mary," said Henny, "I know what I'd like to do. I'd like to stay in Saltmouth. It's all been so wonderful—yesterday afternoon, sitting on the sand, and then that marvelous supper you made, and going up the stairs to that lovely little apartment—like a child climbing into a treehouse—and having a room to myself. At the Home I had to share with a couple of other old ducks who snored and quacked in their sleep. Oh, I haven't felt so carefree since I was Angela's age."

"Have you not had a happy life, then, Henny?" asked Mary Good.

"Mustn't complain, I suppose," said Henny, "but I spent most of it looking after my parents. Mother was a bit of an invalid, and Father never did a lot, so I stayed home and kept house for them. Housework! Well, you'd know all about that in a big place like this. Cooking for seven, to start with. That must take up a lot of your time."

"Yes, but I like cooking. It's my hobby, I suppose."

"What about all the dusting and cleaning?"

"Oh, I don't like that."

"Sewing? Mending?"

"I'm hopeless at that."

"Ironing?"

"Ugh! Horrible!"

"Polishing the brass and the silver? Getting between the tines of all the forks?"

"Oh, stop it, Henny!" cried Mary Good. "I hate all those jobs. Of course very few people employ servants nowadays, but I remember that my grandparents had a live-in servant to do all those sorts of things. A housekeeper."

"Mary," said Henny. "I may not be as young as I was, but I can still do all those sorts of things. How would you like to have a housekeeper?"

"She said *what*?" cried George Good when he came home for his lunch. Henny and the five children had all gone down to the beach for a picnic.

"'How would you like to have a housekeeper?'" said Mary Good. "Those were her words."

"I was right," said her husband. "She *is* mad. How can anyone suddenly become a domestic servant at the age of seventy-five? She couldn't possibly do the work. Anyway, we don't need to employ anyone. You've always managed perfectly well on your own, haven't you?"

"Yes."

"And you've always said you don't want a stranger in your house?"

"Yes."

"Well, Henny's strange enough, I should think. Don't tell me you're actually thinking of agreeing to this harebrained idea?"

"I'd like you to consider it, George," said his wife.

"Consider it? I consider it crazy. Where's she going to live, for starters?"

"In the apartment."

"In the apartment? What about when your parents come to visit? Or mine?"

"That little room with a single bed is no use to either set of grandparents, you know that. They always go in the big spare room."

"But think of the value of that apartment.

33

Here in Saltmouth in the season, we could rent that to someone for a lot of money."

"But we don't want to, do we?"

"Yet you want that old woman to live in it. Rent-free, I suppose? And what about the expense of her wages when she starts playing at being a housekeeper?"

"Henny will write to the Home and ask them to forward her pension money, explaining that she is staying with friends indefinitely."

"Friends? Indefinitely?"

"And then each week we will take some of her pension for her bed and board and she'll keep the rest for her spending money. Just think of it, George, from my point of view. No more ironing, no more silver cleaning, no more mending the children's clothes or sewing on buttons—all things that a fit seventy-five-year-old can easily do. And a permanent babysitter whenever we want to go out in the evening. Don't you think we should give the idea a try? Just for a month, say?"

"I knew it, I knew it!" said George Good. "I told you so, didn't I? I said that's what you'd say—'just for a night, just for a week'—and now it's 'just for a month.' You and your soft heart. You must be soft in the head, too. Quite apart from the pros and cons of this crazy scheme, we don't know anything at all about Miss Henrietta Hickathrift."

"I like her," said Mary Good. "I like her very much. And the children think she's marvelous. But of course if you say no to the idea, then no it must be."

The dentist shook his balding head irritably, like a cornered bull.

"I haven't said no," he replied.

"That makes things much easier," said his wife before he could continue, "because I've already said yes."

4

On the beach Henny and the Good children were picnicking. They had gone down early to secure their favorite spot before any vacationers could get it.

It was in a narrow triangular cleft between two big rocks at the base of the cliffs. Once they had parked themselves there, no one else could get in, and they thought of this little patch of sand with its rocky walls as a kind of second home. At the back of it there was actually a small cave, in which, if it rained, they could seek cover.

The children would throw their belongings around and drape their towels on the rocks, and when they went down the beach to play or to swim, they would barricade the entrance to their chosen place with shovels and buckets. Barney had made a sign out of cardboard and attached strings so that it could be hung on a shovel. He had let Rowley write on it with a big red felt pen. It said:

KEP OUT!

This morning the children had swum already. Angela was a strong swimmer, ready to act as lifeguard if anyone needed help. Barney swam well, Eleanor quite well, Rosie a bit, and Rowley splashed about with his water wings on. Henny took off her shoes and stockings, rolled up her skirt, and went wading.

Now everyone was very hungry, so they decided to have the picnic early. The Goods' picnics were always the same—sandwiches and fruit. Each child had an apple and a banana, but the sandwiches varied from picnic to picnic, according to whose turn it was to choose what should be in them.

If it was Angela's turn, for example, she always chose cheese, and so they all had cheese sandwiches. Barney always chose peanut butter; Eleanor, Spam; Rosie, strawberry jam; and Rowley, honey sandwiches.

On this day it had been Eleanor's turn.

"So it's Spam," said her mother.

"No," said Eleanor.

"You want a change? You always have Spam."

"No. Let Henny choose," said Eleanor.

"Good girl," her mother said. "Henny, what's your favorite sandwich?"

"Oh, I don't think I'd better tell you," said Henny. "They'd be too much trouble to make and the children might not like them. No, I'd better not say."

"Oh, go on, Henny!" they all cried.

"Well, it's prawn and mayonnaise. I had one on the train coming here, and it was delicious."

"No trouble," said Mary Good, "and I'm sure the children will like them."

"I won't," said Rowley.

But when it was time to eat, he bolted his sandwiches like a wolf.

"Nice, Rowley?" asked Henny.

"All right."

"Nicer than honey?" asked Rosie.

"He would probably have liked a prawn and mayonnaise and honey sandwich," said Barney.

"I would," said Rowley. "Can I have ice cream now?"

No one answered.

When the children's parents were there, they could usually be persuaded to treat them. Rowley in particular believed that grownups had a duty to provide ice cream.

"Can I, Henny?" he asked again. "Please?"

"Who's going to pay for it?" said Henny.

"You are."

"I've only got a penny."

"And I haven't brought any money with me," said Angela.

"Nor I," said the other three.

Rowley sighed, shaking his head.

"You know, Henny, you'll have to earn some money," he said. "You'll have to get a job." And he took the KEP OUT! sign off his shovel and went to dig a hole.

"As a matter of fact," Henny said to the others, "I've got one. I got it this morning before we came down to the beach."

"That's wonderful!" said Angela. "What job have you gotten?"

"Housekeeper."

"Housekeeper?" they cried. "What does that mean? What will you have to do?"

"Oh, some cleaning, some ironing, some mending, that sort of thing."

"But where?"

"Here in Saltmouth."

"Whereabouts?"

"Place called Ivy Cottage."

There was a pause of perhaps three seconds while this sank in. Then the four older children let out a whoop of delight.

"That's marvelous!" said Angela.

"That's great!" said Barney.

"Excellent!" said Eleanor.

"Cool!" said Rosie.

Rowley, busy digging, had not properly understood.

"I just wish I could have ice cream," he kept muttering.

"And so you shall," said Henny. "Angela, where's the nearest place that sells them?"

"There's a café," said Angela. "Over there. But Henny, you haven't got any money."

"Don't worry about that," said Henny. "You just stay here and look after the others. I won't be long."

As she walked along the beach, Henny remembered another of her mother's many sayings—honesty is the best policy—and when she reached the café, she said to the owner, "I want six large ice cream cones, please, but I think I should warn you that this is all the money I have." And she took from her purse that last penny and put it on the counter.

The man stared at her (very directly, Henny noted).

"Are you asking me," he said, "to give you £3 worth of ice cream for a penny?"

"Yes," said Henny.

She unstrapped her wristwatch and handed it to him.

"You keep this," she said, "until I can pay you. It's old but reliable, like me. I have an honest face, wouldn't you say?"

The man looked more closely still at this odd little gray-haired woman and thought—as people often did of Henrietta Hickathrift—that he had seldom seen such an open, friendly, and honest face.

"Which flavor would you like, madam?" he said.

"Strawberry!" shouted Rowley when Henny arrived back, three pink ice cream cones in each hand. "Yum!"

"But how—?" began Angela.

Henny winked at her.

"Ask me no questions," she said, "and I'll tell you no lies. As Mother used to say."

Rowley took a long lick at his ice cream.

"How old's your mother, Henny?" he asked.

"She'd be a hundred this year," said Henny, "if she was still alive."

"Dead, is she?" said Rowley.

"Yes. She died years and years ago. So did my father. I'm not just a stray, I'm an orphan, too!"

"But you're not a stray anymore, Henny," said Angela. "Now that you're going to live with us."

Rowley pricked up his ears.

"Are you?" he said.

"Yes."

"In the apartment?"

"Yes."

"Good," said Rowley happily. "Then you can buy us ice cream every day."

He took another long, slobbery lick.

"Too many sweet things are bad for your teeth," said Henny.

"Dad's always telling us that," said Barney.

"You're lucky, having a dentist for a father," said Henny. "I bet you've all got wonderful teeth."

"We have," said Eleanor.

"Look," said Rosie. She drew back her lips and bared her teeth at Henny, and then the rest did the same.

"Show us yours, Henny," said Rowley.

"Not likely," said Henny. "Mine are ugly old yellow things, those I've got left. I never took proper care of them when I was young."

"Why not?" asked Eleanor.

"Terrified of the dentist."

"Are you frightened of Dad, then?" asked Rosie.

"I would be if I was sitting in his dentist's chair."

"He's ever so gentle," said Barney. "He never hurts us a bit."

"That's because you've all got perfect teeth that don't need anything done to them. I bet he'd hurt me."

"Well, what do you do if you get a toothache?" asked Angela.

"Grin and bear it," said Henny.

She took a mouthful of her ice cream.

"Ooh, it's cold!" she said.

Then suddenly she gave a little jump and clapped a hand to her cheek.

"Ow!" she cried.

5

Aching

Oh! said Henny quietly to herself for the umpteenth time. Twenty-four hours had gone, but the toothache hadn't.

She had begged some aspirin from Mary Good, saying she had a headache, but it hadn't helped. As usual, one of the late Mrs. Hickathrift's many sayings came to mind—"What can't be cured must be endured"—but the sudden shooting pain in a big back tooth was now even more frequent.

Nonetheless, Henny determinedly began her duties at Ivy Cottage, hoping that work would take her mind off her troubles. She had persuaded the children's mother to go down to the beach with them (Spam sandwiches, Eleanor's turn now) and was tackling a huge pile of ironing.

When it felt like eleven, she felt like a cup of

tea and looked at her wrist, only to remember where her watch now was, and when she'd made the tea, the first sip of it made her tooth jump like anything. In fact, by the time George Good came home for his lunch, Henny hardly knew what to do with herself, so constant was the sharp nagging pain.

But I mustn't show it, she thought. She remembered her last visit to a dentist, half a lifetime ago, especially the awful buzzing of the drill inside her mouth.

"All alone, then?" said today's dentist.

"Yes. They've all gone down to the beach. Your lunch is ready."

"Aren't you going to have some?"

"No, I don't feel like eating, thank you."

"You're not ill?"

"No, no, I'm fine," said Henny, and at that instant the pain stabbed at her viciously, as though to punish her for telling such a whopper.

"Oh! Oh!" she cried, clapping both hands on one side of her face.

"I don't have to be a dentist," said George Good, "to tell that you have a toothache. Haven't you?"

Henny nodded.

"Well, you've come to the right place. As it happens, I've got a cancellation this afternoon. I can fit you in."

Henny shook her head.

"No? Why not?"

"I'm terrified of going to the dentist. I always have been."

"When did you last have your teeth checked?"

"About thirty years ago," said Henny. "I shall never forget it. Oh, that awful drill, I can hear it now. And I had to have two out as well, and he gave me gas, it was so nasty, the smell of it, and I went all woozy and I could hear sort of funny music inside my head, oh, it was all so horrible!"

"Look, Henny," said George Good, "things are different these days. I wouldn't dream of giving you gas, and I promise you I won't hurt you at all. The worst you'll have to put up with may be a little injection of a local anesthetic, a tiny pin-prick, you won't even feel it."

"I don't believe you."

"Try it and see."

"No. Anyway, I can't afford it."

"Don't worry about that. Let's do something about that toothache."

"It may go away."

"And it may not. Now, do you know where my office is? It's not far."

"Yes. We walked past it yesterday on our way to the beach. Angela pointed it out to me. I shuddered just looking at it."

George Good smiled.

"I've seen lots of frightened patients in my time," he said, "but they're all pleasantly surprised in the end. You be down at the office at three thirty."

Henny grasped at one last straw.

"I can't," she said. "I can't leave the house until the others come back."

"That's easily fixed," said the dentist. "We'll use the Patented Good Emergency Recall Method. Come and watch."

Henny followed him as, armed with a pair of binoculars and a large whistle, he walked down the Ivy Cottage lawn to the sea wall. First he raised the binoculars and scanned the beach.

"Right, they're in the usual spot," he said.

Then he put the whistle to his mouth and blew seven loud blasts.

"Peep-pip-pip-peep-peep! Peep! Peep!"

Quite a number of vacationers, Henny could see, turned their heads at this noise, but then, seeing nothing out of the ordinary, lost interest in what it might mean. But from the cleft in the rocks a figure came out and began to run along the beach toward the harbor. It was Barney. He ran up the ramp that led to the harbor and then along the jetty, until he stood, panting, directly below them.

"What's the matter, Dad?" he called up.

His father leaned over the wall.

"Ask Mom if she'll have you all back here by three fifteen, will you?"

"Why?"

"Henny has an appointment with me at three thirty. Okay?"

"Okay," said Barney.

"Okay?" said his father to Henny.

Henny opened her mouth to say "No," and as she did so, she felt the sharpest stab of pain yet.

Here's a kind man offering to take this pain away, she thought, and you keep refusing his help, you old fool, you. Forget about "What can't be cured must be endured." How about "Don't look a gift horse in the mouth"? Or, rather, "Don't stop a gift dentist from looking in *your* mouth."

"Okay," she said. "I'll come. But I can't guarantee that I won't run away again when I get to the door."

"I don't think you will," said George Good, and before he left the house, he wrote a note to his wife and sealed it in an envelope.

"Give this to Mary when she gets back, will you, Henny, please?" he said.

Mary [it read],
Henny is suffering from a bad toothache and a fear of dentistry. I can see her at three thirty. Don't let her back out on me. Escort her to my office, all of you, and shove her in. I'll do the rest.

George

✳   ✳   ✳

George was right, thought Henny as she climbed into bed that night. He didn't hurt me at all.

At three fifteen the others had arrived home from the beach, and Mary Good had read the note and then showed it to her children while Henny was out of the room. Angela and Barney read it, and then Eleanor read it to Rosie (who couldn't read her father's handwriting) and to Rowley (who couldn't read).

At three twenty-five they all said, "Are you ready, Henny?"

"Ready for what?" said Henny.

"For your appointment."

"Oh, that. I don't think I'll bother."

"We'll all come with you," Mary Good said. "Off we go."

Even at the office door Henny had not given up all hope of escape. But when she turned around, it was to face a solid wall of six Goods.

"In you go," said Mary, ringing the bell.

"There's nothing to worry about," said Angela.

"Like I said, he's ever so gentle," said Barney.

"And the chair's ever so comfy," said Eleanor. "It lets right down like a bed."

"And there's a nice big picture to look at on the ceiling," said Rosie.

"And there's music playing," said Rowley. "Old-fashioned stuff."

Bach? wondered Henny. Brahms? Beethoven?

"What sort of music?" she asked.

"The Beatles," said Rowley.

At that moment the office door opened and there stood a smiling woman who said, "Good afternoon, Miss Hickathrift." Then before Henny knew it, she was inside.

Lying in bed now in the little apartment, Henny pinched her cheek and her lip. Both had gone numb from the local anesthetic, so that they felt fat and she thought she must be talking oddly. Now the numbness had disappeared, and much, much more important, the beastly toothache had gone completely. Though the tooth was still there. George had repaired it.

"Don't want you to lose any more than you already have," he had said when he'd finished. "We won't do anything else today, but there's quite a bit that needs doing. If you don't mind, that is?"

And to her surprise Henny heard herself saying, "No, I don't mind."

Once he'd given me the injection, she thought now (and to be honest, I never even felt it), and when I found nothing was hurting me, I actually almost began to enjoy it. Lying back in that comfortable chair, looking up at that picture of a beach, but not one like Saltmouth—a palm-fringed Caribbean beach of golden empty sands and brilliantly blue seas—and listening to "Michelle" and hearing George's deep voice rumbling on above me, telling me little stories about this and that and occasionally asking me a question that I couldn't answer with my mouth stuck open. I really believe I'm not scared of the dentist anymore—at least not this one. He's a good dentist, he is. And then she smiled and said out loud, "He's a *Good* dentist!"

And then she went to sleep.

6
BOMBING

One evening when the children were all in bed and Henny had just said good night and gone off to climb the stairs to the apartment, Mary said to George, "The month is up."

"What month?" said George.

"Henny's trial month. Remember, you agreed we'd give it a try, see how it worked out?"

"I didn't agree to anything," said George. "You bulldozed me into it."

"Are you sorry?"

"No. It seems to be working out quite well. As long as you're happy about it, Mary?"

"I certainly am. She does such a lot, you know. All that silver and brass cleaning, and the mending, and she irons quite beautifully, oh, and a hundred and one other things she does without being asked. I've got so much spare time now, I'm actually thinking of taking a college course. I wonder how I ever managed without my house-keeper. Though that's a silly thing to call her."

"Home help?"

"Well, yes. Or companion, perhaps. She's not any sort of a servant. She's become a friend. And I'm sure she's happy here. Not the least thanks to you."

"Me?"

"Yes. All that dental work you've done on her, now that she's not scared anymore. What have you charged her for it?"

The dentist stroked his balding head, looking faintly embarrassed.

"Not a lot," he said.

His wife smiled at him.

"Nothing, you mean," she said.

"Well, she hasn't exactly got money to throw about. She only has her pension, and then she has to pay you for her bed and board, though I don't know how much you charge her."

The dentist's wife ran a hand through her fair hair. She looked just a trifle flustered.

"Not much," she said.

Her husband grinned at her.

"Nothing, you mean," he said.

"Well, she's had a lot of expenses lately. Clothes, for example—I had to persuade her to replace that old coat and that tea cozy hat, and she needed shoes and so on. And she's always spending money on the children, did you know? Angela tells me that Henny regularly buys them ice cream at the beach café."

The very first thing that Henny had done as soon as she was able to draw her pension again was to go to the café to reclaim her wristwatch.

"Do you remember me?" she said to the owner. "I owe you some money." And she put three pound coins on the counter.

"Indeed I do, madam," said the owner. "But don't forget, you paid a deposit." And he handed her not just the watch but also one penny, which had been her sole worldly wealth when she first arrived in Saltmouth.

"Thank you," said Henny. "Look after the pennies, my mother used to say, and the pounds will look after themselves."

"Are you staying much longer?" asked the café owner.

"I hope so," said Henny.

On that same evening that George and Mary Good had been discussing her, Henny had been lying in bed in the apartment thinking, Goodness! I've been here at Ivy Cottage a month already! And what a lot has happened since I ran away from the Home. And how lucky I am to be living with this family and to have this lovely little room over the garage.

Before she turned out the light, Henny took a last look around.

On the closet door (in which her new clothes were kept) she had taped things that the children had made for her.

Angela had written her a poem:

When we first set eyes on Henny,
she was seventy-five years old.
All she had was just one penny,
but she has a heart of gold.

Barney, his mind on his as yet unfinished Second World War project, had painted her a picture of a battle. Better not do one of soldiers, he thought, since her boyfriend got killed. Instead he had done a graphic and highly colored scene of a bomber with strings of little bombs falling from it, while above it lots of other planes shot at each other.

Eleanor and Rosie had done portraits of her.

Eleanor, who thought that Henny might be self-conscious about her height, had drawn a tall, thin old lady.

Rosie, who drew everyone the same—that is to say the same shape as herself—had drawn her short and fat.

The only similarity between the two portraits was that both were titled *Henny.*

Hanging on the closet doorknob was Rowley's present, a long rope of seaweed.

"You can tell the weather by it," he said.

"How?" asked Henny.

"If the seaweed stays damp and rubbery, then it's going to rain. And if the seaweed turns all dry and hard and crackly, then the weather will be fine."

The seaweed had stayed damp, but the weather remained stubbornly fine.

Mary Good, who was a keen gardener, had given Henny a potted plant.

"It's called *Cressula argentea*," she had said, "the jade tree. But some people call it the money plant."

"Perhaps I'll win the lottery," said Henny.

"Don't overwater it," said Mary. "It doesn't like that. And don't worry if it doesn't do well—I've got loads more of them."

Now it stood in its heavy earthenware pot on the sill of the room's one window, which was directly over the garage door. Henny always slept with the curtains partly open to let in a little light from the streetlight outside. And she kept the window open to let in the fresh sea air.

She took a last look at her poem, her three pictures, her seaweed, and her plant. Then she took from her mouth what was the finest of her presents—from the seventh member of the Good family—a beautiful new set of false teeth, dropped them into a tooth glass beside her bed, and turned out the light.

Henny had grown used to the occasional sounds of Saltmouth's late night traffic passing Ivy Cottage, but the sound that woke her later was an unusual one. It was a kind of scraping sound, of metal on metal, and it seemed to be coming from beneath her window.

Henny got out of bed, went quietly across the room, and looked out. Directly below was a man who seemed to be trying to open the garage door.

Her first thought was that it was George. But why would he want to get the car out at—she looked at her watch—two o'clock in the morning?

She leaned out a little farther and now could see by the light of the streetlight that it was certainly not George.

George was big. This man was smallish.

George was balding. This man had a lot of hair tied in a ponytail.

George had a key to his garage. This man, she could see, had some sort of crowbar in his hand with which he was trying, as quietly as he could, to force open the garage door.

Some old ladies in Henny's position would have screamed or shouted for help, but all Henny felt was anger, anger on behalf of the Good family, *her* family, as she already felt them to be.

This nasty thief was actually trying to break in and steal their car, their beautiful big shining eight-seater monster (she had had a ride in it and knew that it would take seven Goods and one Hickathrift).

What's more, he was trying to steal it right under her nose!

If I give a shout for George, she thought, the man will just run away. And I can't very well sneak down the stairs in my blue flannel night-gown with the pattern of red roses and grab him in a headlock. He may be small, but I'm smaller and a heck of a lot older. Besides, he'd most like-ly knock my teeth out—the ones that aren't in the tooth glass, I mean. What shall I do?

Then her eye fell on Barney's painting of the bomber and then on the money plant at her elbow.

Quickly she picked up the heavy pot and held it out past the window sill.

Carefully, though her arms began to ache with the weight of it, she moved the pot a fraction this way and that—just like a bombsight in an air-plane—till it was, she judged, directly above that ponytailed head below.

Then she dropped it.

7

GAMBLING

At breakfast the next morning the children were told all about the bombing of the burglar.

"I was woken up by the sound of Henny shouting my name," their father said, "and when I got outside, there was this chap knocked out cold. I recognized him straightaway, because he was lying on his back with his mouth open, and when I shone the flashlight on him I could see the repair work I'd done on his upper left four. It was young Freddie Hooper—Hooper the boatman's oldest boy."

"The one with the ponytail, Dad?" asked Barney.

"Yes. He's been in trouble with the police before now."

"Are you going to report him?" asked Angela.

"No. I don't think he'll try breaking into our

garage again. He was so dazed he had no idea what had happened. I told him it was part of our security system. Anyway, there wasn't any damage to the door worth speaking of, only to his head. He had a bump on it the size of a hen's egg."

"Oh, dear!" said Henny. "And I broke your flowerpot too, Mary."

"Don't worry," said Mary. "I've got loads of pots and lots more money plants. I'll give you another one for your room, and then we won't ever need to worry about having the car stolen, thanks to the Patented Hickathrift Antiburglar Bomb."

"We're very grateful to Henny," George said to the rest. "Aren't we?" Everyone cried, "Yes!" and then they all clapped and then they sang "For She's a Jolly Good Fellow!"

Henny looked at the five red-haired children and their tall fair-haired mother and their big balding father and thought what jolly Good fellows *they* all were.

After breakfast, when the dentist had left for his office and the children for school—for the new term had started—Mary said, "Well, Henny, the month is up."

"What month?" said Henny.

"Your trial month. Remember, we agreed to give it a try to see how it worked out?"

"Oh, yes," said Henny.

Oh, no, she thought. Don't tell me she's going to say I've got to go! I couldn't bear to be a stray again.

"Well, what d'you think?" said Mary.

"Think?"

"I mean, is the work too much for you?"

"Oh, no!"

"Are you happy with us?"

"Oh, yes!"

"Well, it's all right, then," said Mary.

"I can stay?" said Henny.

"Couldn't manage without you. Did I tell you I've signed up for a college course? In French. We go to France quite often on vacation, so it'll be useful. I hardly took any French when I was in school, and George took none—he just shouts at them slowly in English. Which reminds me, I must get myself a French dictionary. Oh, and I must go and find you another money plant."

"Speaking of money," Henny said. "I haven't given you any, you know. I must pay for my bed and board. We agreed I should."

"Don't worry about that," said Mary. "You more than earn your keep with all the work you do. By the way, could you do a bit of shopping for me this morning? Nothing heavy."

In the town Henny collected the few little things on Mary's list. One of them was a lottery ticket, and just for luck Henny got one for herself as well. Then she treated herself to a box of jujubes.

As she sucked one of these, held between her new teeth, she had a brainstorm. I've got quite a lot of money now, she thought, because Mary won't take any. But she can't stop me from buying her a present. And she made her way to a bookshop.

"Just look at this!" said Mary Good to her husband when he came home for lunch, and she put before him a very large new dictionary, on whose shiny cover was written:

FRENCH–ENGLISH

ANGLAIS–FRANÇAIS

George picked it up, looked at the price on it, and gave a whistle.

"Twenty quid!" he said. "You've gone all out!"

"Look inside," said his wife.

On the flyleaf was written:

TO MARY GOOD

FROM HENRIETTA HICKATHRIFT

Henny came into the room.

"How very generous of you, Henny," said George, brandishing the heavy book.

"It's you two that are generous to me," said Henny. "I only wish there was some way I could repay you for your kindness."

Perhaps I could win some money with this thing, she thought later. She was sitting on a chair outside Ivy Cottage, her lottery ticket in her lap, watching the evening sun on the sea. I wonder what you have to do? The children will know.

The children were playing croquet on the lawn. It was a very special and difficult sort of croquet, because the slope meant that the croquet balls all tended to roll down toward the sea wall, and anyway, that's where the players tried to knock one another. It was also a dangerous game, as Henny had found out on the one and only occasion on which she had played, because everyone hit the croquet balls as hard as they could and your ankles were in great danger.

When the game was finished, four of them came up the lawn toward her, red heads bright in the evening sun.

Barney was grinning because he had won.

Angela was smiling because she didn't mind not having won.

Eleanor and Rosie were quite happy because they never won anyway.

Behind them Rowley was still playing all by himself. He placed the ball right in front of each hoop and then knocked it through, the only way he ever scored anything.

"Tell me," said Henny to the four older ones. "Do you know how to do this lottery thing?"

"I do," said Angela. "I've seen Mom do it. You have to choose six numbers between one and forty-nine. That costs you a pound. Then when it comes to the draw, if you've got the first five numbers that they call out, you can win an awful lot of money."

Rowley arrived in time to hear this.

"Seventy million pounds," he said. "A man did."

"Seven*teen* million," the others said.

"I don't think I'd want to win that much," Henny said. "I wouldn't know what to do with it."

"Give it to us," said Rowley.

"I have to choose six, did you say?" asked Henny.

"Yes."

"Well, look, there's me and there's the five of you. Let's each pick a number. Start with the youngest. What number d'you want, Rowley?"

"Five," said Rowley. "Because that's what I'm going to be, soon."

Then the rest made a choice, in turn, and each time Henny made against the chosen number a clean vertical line with a ballpoint pen, as the instructions said.

"There we are, then," she said at last. "Five,

twenty-five, thirty-one, thirty-nine, forty-four."

"Six," said Angela. "You have to pick six numbers, Henny. What are you going to pick?"

"Oh, I don't know. Let's see, I'll say thirteen."

"That's unlucky," said Rowley.

"Which is what I shall be, Rowley, you can bet your bottom dollar," said Henny. "I never win these sorts of things. Waste of a pound, really."

8

RESCUING

When Saturday night came, they were all glued to the television to watch the draw for the lottery.

"If you win," George Good said to his wife, "do I get half?"

"Certainly not," she said. "I paid for the ticket, and I chose the numbers, and I'm going to spend the millions."

"We all chose Henny's numbers," said Angela.

"I chose five, Dad," Rowley said. "Did you choose five, Mom?"

"No."

"You should have," said Rowley. "It will come up, it will. I bet you my bottom dollar."

And sure enough it did.

"Number five!" read out the woman on the television.

"Yes!" cried the four older children.

"Told you," said Rowley.

But that was it.

All of Mary's numbers were wrong, and of Henny's the only correct one was Rowley's five.

"You better let me pick them all next time," he said.

"I don't think I'll bother again," said Henny, but even as she said it, she heard her mother's voice saying "If at first you don't succeed, try, try again."

The next day they all went down to the beach together. Now, with the vacationers all gone, the sands were comparatively empty and the Goods' chosen place needed no KEP OUT! notice to protect it. As an added bonus, the mid-September weather was still fine and the sea still fairly warm, so the family swam.

"Who's for a nice long walk, right to the far end of the beach?" asked George afterward, and everyone was except Henny, who said she'd rather sit and watch the sea, and Rowley, who wanted to finish digging a large grave for a dead jellyfish he'd found.

"I'll look after Rowley," Henny said, so the others set off without him.

Sitting comfortably in the sunshine, listening to the gentle hiss and slap of the waves and the cries of the gulls, Henny watched the walkers gradually growing smaller as they made their way along the beach toward the distant headland.

When they were no more than dots, she opened a book, but after a while she felt her eyes grow heavy and found that she was reading the same sentence again and again. She took off her glasses and put them in their case, closed the book, and promptly went to sleep.

She was awakened by the sound of a child's voice yelling. It sounded like Rowley's. She looked around. The dead jellyfish lay in its now completed grave, waiting to be buried, but there was no sign of Rowley.

Scrambling hastily to her feet, Henny strained her eyes in the direction of the yells, which were coming from the sea. Her heart in her mouth, she hurried down the beach and saw, quite a ways out—out of his depth, certainly—a small figure that splashed wildly and shouted loudly—in terror, it seemed to her. Every now and then the figure would disappear beneath the surface to emerge again shouting and splashing even more frantically.

He's drowning! Henny thought. He's gone in without his water wings and he's gone out too far and he's drowning. And without hesitation she plunged out toward the boy.

"I'm coming, Rowley!" she called. "Henny's coming!" And determinedly she waded on out until, up to her neck now, she grabbed hold of a flailing arm and began to drag the child shoreward.

"Let go of me! Leave me alone!" the boy kept shouting.

"It's all right, Rowley, it's all right!" panted Henny.

Not until she reached the shallows, breathless and soaked to the skin, did she find that without her glasses she had made a slight mistake.

Suddenly she heard an angry man's voice saying, "What d'you think you're up to? Kindly let go of my son immediately!"

"Oh, dear," said Henny, peering at the strange child. "I thought he was someone else and I thought he was drowning."

"Drowning?" said the man. "He swims like a fish!"

"But he was shouting and splashing."

"Children do," said the man, "when they're allowed to enjoy themselves without interfering old ladies grabbing hold of them."

"I'm sorry," said Henny, dripping.

"Busybody!" said the man.

Henny trudged back up the beach until she was close enough to see that Rowley was just completing his work, patting down the little mound that now covered the body of the late lamented jellyfish. He looked up.

"You're wet," he said.

Then there was a thudding of feet as the other Goods, returning from their walk, caught sight of the bedraggled Henny and came running.

"Henny!" they cried. "Whatever's happened?"

Henny managed a smile.

"I heard a child calling," she said. "In the sea. I thought it was Rowley."

"And you thought he was in trouble?" asked George.

"Yes."

"And you went in to rescue him?" asked Mary.

"Yes. But it wasn't him. It was another little boy, and he wasn't in trouble at all. I didn't have my specs on, you see."

"But surely," they said, "Rowley was right here beside you?"

"No, he wasn't. I dropped off to sleep, you see, and when I was awakened—by a child yelling—I couldn't see him anywhere, so I thought it was him in the sea."

"It was terribly, terribly brave of you, Henny," said Mary Good. "You're coming straight home with me now this minute." And she put a big towel around Henny's shivering shoulders and led her away.

When they had gone, George Good said to his youngest child, "If all this happened because Henny couldn't see you, Rowley, where were you, then? Did you go off somewhere by yourself?"

"Only for a minute," Rowley said. "Henny was asleep. She didn't notice."

"Where did you go, then?"

"Into the cave."

"Why?"

"I had to go to the bathroom."

9

AILING

The next day it was plain that Henny was not at all well. Whether or not it had to do with her soaking, she developed a cough and said she felt achy, and Mary Good put her to bed in the apartment and called a doctor.

"She's got a bit of a temperature," the doctor said afterward. "I'll give you a prescription for antibiotics for her."

In their different ways all the children felt Henny's absence.

Rowley missed her because he was the only one with whom she would play croquet—he could not hit as dangerously hard as the others, and also she let him have two shots to her one.

Eleanor and Rosie missed her because she read to them. Each was in fact a good reader, but

it's very nice just to sit and listen to someone else, especially if they read well, with all the proper different voices, which Henny did.

Barney was no longer able to ask her questions about the Second World War. She couldn't of course tell him about the fighting, but she had lived in London during the Blitz and knew all about the doodlebug bombs and the V-2 rockets. He hadn't liked to ask much about her boyfriend, but she had told him that he had been a guardsman by the name Matthew Strong and that he had been killed in the invasion at Salerno in Italy.

Angela, as the oldest, was best able to appreciate Henny's many skills—as a needlewoman, for example: Angela's first effort at a piece of embroidery was at a stage where she needed Henny's advice.

All five children missed their friend. In some funny way she seemed to them to have lived at Ivy Cottage forever.

"Unfortunately," said Mary to her husband the next morning, "as well as feeling ill, she's feeling guilty."

"Guilty? About what?"

"About dropping off to sleep when she was meant to be watching Rowley."

"But there was no harm done."

"But there might have been, she keeps saying to me. 'It might have been Rowley in the water, and I might not have heard him in time.' Anyway, I've got the doctor coming again today. I don't think these antibiotics are working. Her temperature is still sky high, and she's beginning to ramble a bit. I listened outside the door just now and she was saying 'Matthew! Matthew! It's all right! Henny's coming!' Who could Matthew be? A relative? We don't even know if she has any relatives. What happens if . . ."

"If what?"

"If she gets worse, and we need to contact someone in her family?"

"Well," said George. "That old age home she was in, they'd know, if anyone would. Do you have their number?"

"Yes."

"Let's phone them, then."

So they did and were told only that Henny

had a sister in Birmingham. She had said so in a note that she had left.

The Goods then called friends of theirs who lived in Birmingham and asked them to look through the local telephone directory to see if there was a Hickathrift listed. There wasn't.

"Anyway," said Mary, "it could have been a married sister."

"She'll have to be admitted to the hospital," said the doctor when he came. "She has pneumonia, there's not much doubt about it. How old did you say she was?"

"Seventy-five."

"Hmm. Her heart's all right. We'll just have to see."

The children watched in silence as the ambulance workers maneuvered the stretcher down the stairs from the apartment and loaded Henny into the ambulance for the trip to the hospital. Her eyes were open, but it was plain she recognized none of them, and as the stretcher passed them she said again, "Matthew! It's Henny, I'm coming!"

As they watched the ambulance disappear, the

children's father asked, "Has Henny ever talked to any of you about someone named Matthew?"

"Yes, me, Dad," said Barney.

"A brother, is he? A cousin, perhaps?"

"No, her boyfriend was named Matthew. The one that got killed in the war, in 1943."

In the afternoon Mary went to the hospital.

"How is she?" asked George when he arrived home from his office.

"Oh, George, I don't much like the look of things. She didn't recognize me, and she's got this terrible cough. And her temperature hasn't come down—I looked at her chart. They're trying a different antibiotic now and putting it directly into a vein in her arm. Perhaps it was partly because the women in the beds on either side were large, but Henny just looked so *small*."

The children came in from playing croquet.

"How's Henny?" they asked. "Is she better?"

"Well, no," said Mary. "I wouldn't say better. Not yet. But she's in the best place to get better. It's a very good little hospital. They'll make her well."

At the hospital Mary had been asked for Henny's personal details.

"Name?"

"Henrietta Hickathrift."

"Age?"

"Seventy-five."

"Address?"

"She lives with us—Ivy Cottage, St. Edmund's Street."

"Next of kin?"

"None that we know of."

"She's not related to you, Mrs. Good?"

"No. Just a friend, I'll give you my phone number in case you need to contact me. I'll be in tomorrow morning."

For some reason the phone seemed to ring a lot in Ivy Cottage that evening, and Mary Good, sitting by it, picked it up each time hoping against hope that it would not be the hospital calling. They won't bother to contact me if there's any improvement, she said to herself, only if she's worse, or if she has . . . Suddenly she realized what a dreadful thing Henny's death would be for them all. Yet she had only been a part of their lives such a short time.

But the phone calls were all from family or

friends, none of whom had ever set eyes on Henrietta Hickathrift.

By the next day there was no change in Henny's condition. George, who visited at lunchtime, spoke with the consulting physician, who happened to be a friend with whom he played golf.

"What are her prospects, Charles?" he asked.

"Well," said the consultant, "it's a very nasty pneumonia, George, and her temperature is still very high. The trouble is, if we can't get it down soon, she may well start hallucinating, and that will not be pleasant. Is she a relative of yours?"

"No. She just turned up on our doorstep. She'd run away from home—an old age home to be exact—and my children brought her to our house. They'd seen this message that she'd written in the sand with her cane: 'I am a stray old woman.' She's turned out to be a very remarkable old woman, and we've all become very fond of her. We've adopted her, I suppose you could say. I just hope to goodness you can pull her through, Charles."

"The next couple of days will tell."

That night the long spell of good weather finally broke, and it rained from dusk to dawn. In Henny's bedroom, Rowley's rope of seaweed, which had remained damp and rubbery, had now turned dry and crackly. As she was dusting the next afternoon, Mary considered throwing the dead-looking stuff away, but then she thought, No, I can't, it's Henny's. She'd notice if it was gone when she comes back . . . if she comes back.

After tea, the four older children were doing their homework. The rain had stopped, and Rowley, wearing his galoshes, was playing croquet against himself on the lawn. Deprived of Henny as an opponent, he had invented a new method in which he played using two different croquet balls, red against blue, taking alternate shots. This way he always won.

His game over, he raised his mallet with a shout of triumph and trudged back up the lawn just as his father arrived home.

"Dad," he said. "When is Henny coming out of that hospital?"

"Soon, I hope, Rowley," George said. "I'm going there this evening to see how she is."

"Can I come with you?"

George Good considered. Angela and Barney, he knew, realized that Henny was dangerously ill and that she might possibly die, and even Eleanor and Rosie had some idea, he felt, of how serious things were.

Rowley, though, was simply waiting for her to come home, expecting her to come home, and it had never occurred to him that she might not.

Should he take him in to see her? Then he might understand how ill she was. Maybe then it wouldn't be such a shock to him if she did die. Henny wouldn't know the boy, of course. She hadn't recognized anybody for days now. But each of the other children had visited, just for a few moments. Only Rowley had not.

"All right," he said. "You can come with me."

"How is Miss Hickathrift?" George asked the nurse at the door of the ward. I don't want to walk in and find an empty bed, he thought.

"A little better, you'll be pleased to hear, Mr. Good," said the nurse. "Her temperature is down—only a point or so, but that's what we want to see—and she's breathing more easily. She should be clearer in her mind now, too."

"That's marvelous!" the dentist said.

"At the moment," said the nurse, "she's sleeping peacefully, so it's probably best not to wake her."

"We'll be as quiet as mice," said George. "Won't we, Rowley?"

Rowley nodded.

They sat silently beside Henny's bed, and George, looking at her, thought, not for the first time, that he had seldom seen such an open, friendly, and honest face as hers. Her mouth was slightly open as she slept, and it was with satisfaction that George saw the glint of those new teeth. Once she's well again, I'll do some more work on her, he thought. I don't think I've got the bite quite right.

It was then that Rowley sneezed.

Henny opened her eyes.

"Bless you!" she said. And then, "Why, it's Rowley! And George! I'm not dreaming, am I?"

"No," said George. "You haven't been very well, Henny. But you're certainly looking better today."

"How long have I been in this place?"

"Three days."

Henny shook her head.

"I've been in such a muddle," she said. "All sorts of funny thoughts in my head."

She put out a hand toward Rowley and he took it.

"Bong jooer," he said.

"Before long," said George, "you'll be coming home with us, Henny."

"Home," said Henny softly.

"One of the things my mother is always saying," said George, "is 'East, west, home is best.'"

"Funny," said Henny. "My mother always said that too."

She yawned.

"Oh, I'm tired," she said.

"You go back to sleep," said George. "Mary will visit in the morning. We'll say good-bye for now."

"Good-bye," said Henny.

"Oh rev-wah," said Rowley.

10

WISHING

"Two things, George," said the dentist's consultant friend when the time came for Henny to be discharged from the hospital. "One, your Miss Hickathrift will need some time to recover. She's had a nasty illness, and it'll be at least a month before she feels fit to do much. And the second thing is, are you fit for a round of golf on Saturday?"

Back in Ivy Cottage, Henny did indeed feel a bit weak.

"It's as though I'd been run over by a steamroller," she said, and she was glad of a helping hand from Angela or Barney to get her up the wooden stairs to the apartment at each day's end.

Mary Good would not allow her to do any work harder than sewing on a button and encouraged her to ask for her favorite things to eat and drink "to build up your strength," she said.

"I remember," said Henny, "that once when I was ill as a child, my mother gave me beef tea."

"Beef tea you shall have," said Mary.

The consultant was right. Not until about a month after leaving the hospital did Henny begin to feel like her old self again. Then one morning Mary found her busy cleaning the insides of all the windows.

"Don't overdo it, will you?" she said.

"It's you that's been overdoing it," said Henny. "What with George and all the children to look after and me on top of that. You've had no time even to start on your French class. You need a break. Get George to take you away."

"Where to?" Mary said.

"France, of course. Spend a couple of nights in Paris."

Mary laughed.

"I do have five children, you know," she said.

"Yes," said Henny, "and you've got me. Am I not to be trusted with the children?"

"Of course! But you've been ill . . ."

"And now I'm better."

Mary did put up some sort of resistance, but the thought of the delights of Paris undermined her defenses. Anyway, George jumped at the idea (which Henny suggested to him behind his wife's back), and the children (encouraged by Henny) played their parts.

"Just think of you and Dad strolling down the Champs Élysées," Angela said to her mother.

"And going to the Louvre Museum," said Barney.

"And climbing the Eiffel Tower," said Eleanor.

"And drinking lots of wine," said Rosie.

"And eating frogs' legs!" said Rowley. "Tray bong!"

So it was that during the midterm vacation, Henny and the five Good children had Ivy Cottage all to themselves.

"Are you sure you'll be all right?" George and Mary had said as they left.

They had told their next-door neighbors that they would be away for two nights and that George had given Barney his whistle, with orders to blow it hard if there was any trouble.

"Like that chap with the ponytail?" said Henny.

"Young Freddie Hooper, you mean?" said George. "Oh, you won't need the Patented Hickathrift Antiburglar Bomb, Henny. Freddie's in jail, doing six months for car theft."

And remembering the money plant reminded Mary to give Henny instructions about looking after all her other plants, and that reminded George to tell Henny where the fuse box was in case the power failed, and how to turn the water off in case a pipe burst, and how to regulate the heating, and so on and so forth, until Henny almost had to push them out the door.

"Anyone would think you were going for two months," she said. "Go on, off with you, and have a lovely time."

At the very last moment Mary said, "Oh, I forgot to fill in my lottery ticket. It's in the drawer in the kitchen table."

"Too late now," George said. "We shall miss our train. Come on, the taxi's here."

"Oh, Henny," said Mary. "You fill it in for me, will you?"

She looked in her purse.

"Oh, I haven't got a pound."

"I've got one," Henny said. "I'll see to it. Off you go."

"Good-bye! Good-bye!" everyone called except Rowley, who shouted, "Oh rev-wah!"

After the taxi had disappeared and the children had gone back into the house, Henny stood for a moment outside Ivy Cottage wondering what Paris was like (for she had never in her life been abroad) and hoping that George and Mary would enjoy their break.

Then around the corner of the street came the sweep's van with Mr. Pobjoy, Saltmouth's chimney sweep, at the wheel, his face, as usual, grimy with soot. When you saw a sweep, Henny remembered, you could make a wish. But you mustn't wish until you'd also seen a dog's tail, or the wish wouldn't come true. As if by magic, a dog appeared from a side street, a dog with quite a long tail.

What luck, thought Henny, and then she said out loud, "I wish that George and Mary Good have a really lovely time in Paris."

The dog came closer, nosing about on the pavement, and then Henny recognized it. It was the same thin, collarless mongrel that she had seen on the beach on her very first afternoon in Saltmouth. It's a stray, like me, she had thought then, and by the look of things it still was.

Henny was sure it was the same animal, partly because of its coloring—black, with a white patch on its chest and one white forepaw—but mostly because she remembered it as being different from most dogs. Its ears were not like most dogs' ears. One stuck up, one hung down. It had quite a lot of whippet in it, Henny thought, a bit of terrier, perhaps, maybe a bit of Labrador.

Some mongrels are downright ugly, but this one was rather attractive.

Or you could be, thought Henny, if someone looked after you properly and put some flesh on you. Under its black coat, the dog's ribs showed clearly.

Whether Henny would have done what she did next if George and Mary had still been at home is hard to tell. But, in fact, she darted back into Ivy Cottage, went into the kitchen, and

looked around for something, anything, to offer the hungry animal. Then she remembered. Yesterday they had had sausages and mashed potatoes, and surprisingly, considering the Goods' good appetites, one sausage had been left over. She took it from the fridge and hurried back to the front door.

The black dog was still in sight, although it had moved a little farther up the street.

Henny whistled.

At the sound the dog looked around, one ear cocked, one drooping.

"Here!" called Henny. "Look!" And she held out the sausage.

Cautiously the dog moved closer, muzzle lifted to test the air.

"Poor boy," said Henny. "You haven't just been starved, you've had a few kicks in your time, I reckon. But I won't hurt you. And this will do you good. It's one of Mr. Braintree the butcher's very best pork sausages. Come on, it's all for you. A present from one stray to another."

Drawn by the sight and smell of the food and lulled by the sound of a gentle, friendly voice, the black mongrel forgot his fears, and with a sudden movement snatched the prize from Henny's fingers. In two or three bites he gulped it down, and his long thin tail began to wag slowly.

"Nice?" asked Henny, and the tail wagged faster.

Henny, standing in the open doorway of the house that had become her home, looked at the homeless young dog and was tempted. "While the cat's away," she heard her mother say, "the mice will play." Let's just see if he will come inside, she thought. George and Mary need never know he did. Then I can at least find him a proper meal of something before he goes off to wander about the streets alone again.

The front door of Ivy Cottage had originally been the front door of the middle cottage in the row of three from which the present house had been made. Inside was a longish hallway, with various rooms on either side of it, that led directly to a garden door at the rear of the house. This in turn led to the sloping lawn in the back.

Now, leaving the front door wide open, Henny walked along the hallway, opened the garden door at the far end, then sat down on the seat where she usually sat to watch the children play croquet. The hoops and mallets and balls had all been put away for the winter now, and the lawn was empty except for a couple of seagulls that were walking about on the grass, regarding her with cold yellow eyes.

Henny sat quite still, looking out over the sea wall below. You silly old woman, she said to herself. Did you really imagine he'd follow you, a total stranger?

But then suddenly the seagulls squawked and lifted hastily away from the lawn, and she felt a cold nose nuzzling her hand.

11

Adopting

"Henny! Where are you?"

It was Angela's voice, coming from the hall-way behind.

Henny put a reassuring hand on the black dog's narrow head.

"I'm out here—on the garden seat," she replied.

"Someone left the front door wide open," Angela was saying as she came out of the hall, "so I shut . . ." And then abruptly she stopped both walking and talking as she saw what was sitting beside Henny and gazing up at her.

"Gently," Henny said quietly over her shoulder. "He's probably a bit nervous around people. I don't think he's been very well treated. Go to him slowly. Put your hand out for him to smell."

Angela did as she was told, and the dog

sniffed at her hand and then resumed his fixed stare at Henny.

Angela sat down on the seat beside the two strays.

"Whose dog is he?" she asked.

"I don't know," Henny said. "Nobody's, I think."

Nobody's, I hope, she told herself, for it was already plain that the dog had attached himself to her, and the feeling was mutual.

"What sort of dog is he?"

"Heinz," Henny said.

"What's that mean?"

"Fifty-seven varieties. Which reminds me, I need some proper food for him. I don't want to go myself." (Once he's back out on the street he might just run off, she thought.) "So could you go down to the corner shop and get a can of dog food? Take the money from my wallet—it's in my bag, on the kitchen table."

"Okay."

"Where are the others, by the way?"

"Barney's reading. The rest are playing a game."

"Listen, then, when you come back, tell them about this dog." (Must give him a name, she thought.) "And get them to come out here, not all together, but one at a time, to meet him."

After Angela had gone, Henny sat stroking the black mongrel, trying to decide what to call him. As he sat beside her, the sweep of his tail (on which she had wished) reminded her of seeing sooty Mr. Pobjoy in his van.

Of course, that was the answer! Not Pobjoy—that would be a silly name for a dog—but Sweep!

Angela returned, can in hand.

"Shall I go and open it?" she said.

"Not now," said Henny. "Later. Have you told the others yet?"

"No."

"Well, look, get some of those little crackers out of the jar in the dining room. Get one for each of you to offer to him. Come slowly, quietly, tell them—I don't want him scared."

So in a little while the Good children came through the garden door, one at a time, and went slowly and quietly up to the black dog and gave him a cracker—first Angela, then Barney, then

Eleanor, then Rosie. Last of all Rowley appeared, but there was no cracker in his hand.

"I thought so," Angela said to Henny. And to Rowley she said, "You've eaten it, haven't you? I knew you would. I've brought a spare one. Here you are."

"Here you are," Rowley said to the dog. "What's your name?"

"Sweep," said Henny. "He's called Sweep."

"How d'you know?" said Barney.

"Because I just decided to call him that."

"He's got funny ears, hasn't he?" said Eleanor.

"He's thin, isn't he?" said Rosie.

"He is," said Henny. "You'd better open that can, Angela."

Seldom has a canful of dog food disappeared so quickly into a dog.

Angela put the food into a small bowl. Then they all sat in a row on the garden seat, watching as Sweep threw the meat into himself with a series of convulsive jerks and licked the bowl until it shone.

When at last he raised his head, he looked around at the six faces watching him with a sort of grin on his own and wagged his thanks. Then he lay down at Henny's feet.

"Whose dog is he?" asked Rosie.

"I don't know," said Henny.

"Are you going to keep him?" asked Eleanor.

"I don't know."

I'd like to, Henny thought, but what would George and Mary say? Anyway, he may belong to someone in the town. He may have a perfectly good home of his own. But she felt sure that whatever home he might once have had had not been a perfectly good one.

"He just walked in off the street, did he, Henny?" asked Angela.

"Yes. He followed me."

"I think I've seen him before," Barney said. "There are quite a few dogs like him in the town, just roaming around. They don't seem to belong to anyone. They pick up scraps of food that people drop, and they poke their noses into trash cans. I saw one down by the harbor the other day. One of the boatmen was cleaning fish, and the dog was gobbling up the fish guts. I don't know where they go at night."

I know where this one's going to go tonight if I have my way, thought Henny, and that's on a rug at the foot of my bed.

"I bet," said Barney, "that if you put Sweep back out on the street, he'd just trot off straight through the town looking for food."

"I bet he wouldn't," said Henny.

"How much?"

"Ten pence."

"Done!" said Barney. "Go on! Try it. I'll go up to my bedroom and look out over the street and watch what happens."

"We'll watch too!" cried the others, and off they all ran.

Barney's right, thought Henny unhappily as she got to her feet. This creature's a nomad, a wanderer, a dog of no fixed abode. It's silly of me to think I could just adopt him.

"Come, Sweep," she said with a sigh, and she went through the garden door and along the hallway, the dog at her heels.

When she opened the front door of Ivy Cottage, he showed no sign of wanting to leave. Only when she stepped out onto the pavement, encouraging him to follow, did he do so. Then quickly, feeling very guilty, Henny hopped back inside the house and shut the door in his face.

She stood in the hall listening. She heard a little whine. Then came the scratch of claws on the door. But then there was silence.

For some time Henny stood there, but there was no further sound. He's gone, she thought. I should never have done that to him. I should have made sure he *didn't* get out, not until he was much more settled and sure of himself and of me. Now I've lost him.

Then she heard the children tumbling downstairs, Barney in the lead with a ten pence piece in his hand. He thrust the money into Henny's hand.

"He's just sitting there on the doorstep, waiting!" they cried.

"Shall I open the door?" said Angela, and as soon as she did, Sweep rushed in, making straight for Henny, waggling and wriggling his whole thin body in the joy of being reunited with her.

For the rest of that day he stuck to her like

glue, following her from room to room as she went about the house. He was polite to the children, allowing them to stroke and pat him, but it was plain that it was Henny with whom he had fallen head over heels in love. When she took a bath that evening, he sat outside her bathroom door, and when later, after giving him a last run in the garden, she made her way to bed, Sweep ran up that wooden stairway to the apartment as though he'd climbed stairs all his life.

"Good night, Sweep," said Henny as she turned out her light, and thump, thump, thump went that long black tail on the bedroom floor.

Henny lay awake for a few moments, thinking about all that she'd done that day, in case she'd forgotten anything.

The house had been cleaned, the shopping done (including more cans of dog food), the children had been fed, the dog had been fed, the house was locked up for the night, Barney had George's whistle (and was half longing for an excuse to blow it, Henny thought).

What else? Mary's plants—yes, she'd checked

them. Wait, though! Mary's lottery ticket in the kitchen drawer. She'd forgotten to fill it in.

I'll do it first thing in the morning, Henny thought. But like I said, it's just a waste of a pound. I don't know why I bothered to do it that other time. It's a million to one against winning anything in a sweepstakes like that. *Sweep*stakes! she thought. Maybe *my* Sweep will bring me good luck.

12

WORRYING

As soon as Henny got out of bed the next morning, she opened the door to the apartment and let Sweep run down the stairs into the garden. Because the lawn was fenced on either side, there was no way he could get out, except by leaping over the sea wall (which would have been suicidal), should he wish to escape.

Henny was becoming more and more confident that this was the last thing he wanted to do, but as she dressed, she decided that she must put the matter to the test.

She had no time to fill in Mary's lottery ticket before breakfast, so she stuffed it in her handbag.

After breakfast she said to Angela, "Will you be all right if I go out for half an hour or so? Barney can help you look after the little ones."

"Of course," Angela said. "What about Sweep?"

"I'm taking him with me," said Henny.

"But you haven't got a collar and leash for him."

"I shall buy them at the pet shop."

The pet shop was at the far end of the main street of Saltmouth (and that'll be a good test, Henny thought, to see if he stays with me in spite of other people or other dogs).

She needn't have worried. He stayed as close as he could to her. Does he really need a collar and leash? thought Henny. Yes, of course he does—what if one of the children wanted to take him somewhere? Anyway, a dog should have a collar with its name on it, and she bought him an elegant narrow red one with a leash to match.

"There! Isn't that smart!" she said as they set off again. Sweep seemed to think so. He stepped out jauntily by her side, and there were not a few people in the streets of Saltmouth that morning who smiled at the sight of the happy little old lady and her happy black dog.

When they reached the esplanade, Henny sat down on a bench facing the sea and took off the dog's new collar. On the little brass disk that hung from it she carefully scratched SWEEP with the point of a nail file.

"There you are," she said to him, putting the collar back on. "Now I really feel you're mine. If George and Mary have no objections, that is, though I don't know what I shall do if they have. Even worse, someone might come up and say, 'Hey! What d'you think you're doing with my dog?' But somehow I don't think they will. Come on, let's walk right along to the end and back, and then we must go home."

The houses on the esplanade were all alike, a line of tall, handsome Victorian buildings that had once belonged to wealthy Victorian families. Each carried a brass number on its door.

Once they had all been private dwellings, probably the most desirable in the town because of their nearness to the beach and their views of the sea. But now, Henny noticed as they walked along, almost all of them had been turned into bed-and-breakfasts, each carrying a sign advertising its name. One was called Seaview, and as well there was Balmoral and Gulls' Nest, Welcome House and Costa Brava, Greengables and Clifftops, and many, many more serving the summer vacationers.

When they reached the far end of the esplanade, Henny noticed that the last building in the row was one of the few that had remained a private house. Only its number—1—appeared on the door. Out of interest she counted, on her way back, just how many others had escaped being converted to bed-and-breakfasts.

When she reached the house at the end where she'd started, she found that the answer was six.

Only six out of forty-nine, she thought, and then a sudden thought struck her. She took Mary's lottery card out of her bag and looked at it.

Yes! Each ticket had forty-nine numbers on it. And you had to pick six!

"Stranger things have happened, Sweep," she said. "Let's walk back to the other end once more."

This time as they returned she took a pen from her bag and marked on the lottery card the numbers of the six that were *not* bed-and-breakfasts.

1   6   21   26   31   42

"As good a way of picking as any other, I daresay," she told Sweep. "We'll go into the supermarket on the way home."

Outside the store was a notice that said NO DOGS ALLOWED. GUIDE DOGS ONLY. Henny, confident now of Sweep, tied his leash to a ring in the wall and went in alone.

She handed the card, with that "clean vertical line" through her six chosen numbers, and a pound coin to the woman behind the counter, who put the card into a machine from which it quickly popped out again, and then gave Henny a ticket marked with her numbers.

"I've forgotten," said Henny. "What else do I have to do?"

"Put your name and address on the back," the woman said.

So Henny, without thinking whose ticket it really was, wrote:

> HENRIETTA HICKATHRIFT
> IVY COTTAGE
> ST. EDMUND'S STREET
> SALTMOUTH

* * *

As she had hoped and expected, Sweep was sitting quietly waiting for her, though he greeted her as if they'd been apart for months.

Back at Ivy Cottage, once the new red collar and leash had been admired, Angela said, "Mom and Dad called while you were out."

"Nothing wrong, I hope?" Henny said.

"No, just to say they'll be back tomorrow afternoon. They said they were having a really lovely time."

That's what I wished for, Henny thought. "Anything else?" she asked.

"No. It was a very short call. I asked if they wanted to speak to any of the others, but they said no, they were in a hurry, they were just off to Fontainebleau."

"Did you say anything about Sweep?" asked Henny.

"No, I didn't want to worry them."

"Worry them? You mean they don't like dogs?"

"No, I'm only teasing, Henny," Angela said. "We used to have a dog when I was small and

Barney was a baby, but it died, and since then we've never had another one. Mom's been too busy with all of us, I suppose."

"But Angela, what do you think they'll say?" Henny asked. "About Sweep, and about him sleeping in my room? I mean, I'll buy all his food, he won't cost them a penny, and he's a very clean dog by nature, I'm sure of that, and he's obviously going to be good with you children, and it isn't as though he was a big dog—he doesn't take up much room—and because he's got a smooth coat, he won't leave hairs everywhere, and I'll bet he'll be a good house dog—a dog's the best insurance against burglars, and if I'd had Sweep when that chap with the ponytail tried to break into the garage, he'd have barked and the man would have run away."

She stopped, out of breath.

Angela giggled.

"What's so funny?" said Henny.

"You are. Anyone would think that that dog was the most important person in your life."

Henny looked up at Angela, already so much taller than she, and smiled.

118

"*One* of the most important people," she said.

But the more Henny thought about it, the more she felt that she had not behaved at all well. She was supposed to be acting responsibly while the children's parents were away—she was "*in loco parentis*," and what had she done? Introduced a stray mongrel dog into their house, that's all! So what if they'd owned a dog before and weren't people who didn't like dogs? If they'd wanted another, they'd have gotten one, wouldn't they? Whatever would they think when they arrived home to find that *she'd* gotten one in their absence?

Suppose they said she couldn't keep Sweep? She couldn't bear that. She'd already grown too fond of him. Henny tried to imagine herself saying "If Sweep goes, I go!" But she couldn't bear that, either. She was much too fond of the Goods.

When George and Mary arrived home the following afternoon, and four of their children had said "Hello!" and one had said "Bong jooer," they asked, "Where's Henny?"

"In her room," said Rowley, grinning in a mischievous sort of way.

His parents looked around and saw that the other children were all wearing rather sly, secretive expressions.

"Why is she in her room?" asked their mother.

"She can't be ill," said their father, "or you wouldn't all be looking like Cheshire cats."

"No, she isn't ill," said Rosie.

"What then?"

"She's with her friend," said Eleanor.

"What friend?"

"A sort of boyfriend, I suppose you could call him," said Barney.

"A boyfriend? In her room?"

"She'll be here in a minute," said Angela. "She asked us to sort of prepare the way a bit before she introduced him to you. So you wouldn't be too shocked."

George and Mary Good looked at each other in bewilderment.

Then the door opened and in came Henny and Sweep.

Already in the short time he'd lived at Ivy

Cottage, good feeding had filled him out a little so that his ribs were not so prominent, and Henny had groomed his black coat till it shone, set off by the smart red collar around his neck.

"Sit," said Henny, and Sweep instantly obeyed.

Then before any of the three adults could say a word, a torrent of speech burst from the five children.

"He was a stray!"

"Like Henny!"

"And she rescued him!"

"And he's ever such a good dog!"

"And he's named Sweep!"

"And he sleeps in the apartment!"

"And he's ever so clean!"

"And Henny bought him a collar and leash!"

"And she's going to buy all his food. She says he won't cost you a penny!"

"And he's crazy about her, you can see that!"

"And she's crazy about him!"

George and Mary looked at each other again, and they smiled.

"Well, Henny," said George, "we're very

grateful to you for looking after things. We've had a marvelous time, but it's great to be back with the family once more—all seven of you."

"Seven?" said Angela.

"Yes. You and Barney and Eleanor and Rosie and Rowley and Henny and Sweep."

13
WINNING

What with Paris and Sweep, there was so much to talk about that it was not until the next day, a Saturday, that anyone remembered about the lottery.

"Oh, Henny," said Mary as they all sat around the sitting room fire after lunch. "I forgot to ask . . . Did you remember to fill in my lottery card?"

"Oh, yes," said Henny, "but I forgot to give you the ticket." And she dug in her purse and produced it.

"Thank you," said Mary. "I owe you a pound."

"No, that's all right," said Henny. "Have it on me."

"I wouldn't dream of it. Anyway, it's really the other way around now. You chose the numbers, so it's more your card than mine. But I insist on paying for it."

"No, no," said Henny. "This is your ticket. It's got your name on it."

Mary turned the ticket over. "Actually," she said, "it's got yours, Henny."

"Has it?" said Henny. "Oh, I am silly. The woman in the supermarket said, 'Put your name and address on the back,' and I suppose that's what I did."

"It seems to me, Mary," said George, "that the easiest way is just to leave things as they are. Why don't we say it's Henny's lottery ticket this week, not yours. She paid for it, she chose the numbers, her name's on it."

"Of course," said Mary. "That's the best idea by far. Here, take the card back, Henny—*your* card."

Henny took the lottery card and stood up in front of the fireplace. She held the ticket before her in both hands and, looking hard at Mary, said, "Promise me now, this minute, that if this ticket wins *any* money, you and I will share it between us. Or else I will tear it into pieces and throw them into the fire!"

"Oh, don't do that!" all the children cried.

"Quick, Mary," said Henny, and she made as if to rip the ticket across.

"All right, all right!" Mary laughed. "I promise."

"Saved by the bell," said George. "Tell us, Henny, what numbers have you chosen?"

Henny studied the ticket.

"One, six, twenty-one, twenty-six, thirty-one, and forty-two," she said. "One of them might come up, with a bit of luck, like it did the only other time I've tried, and even that one I didn't choose—Rowley did."

"You should have let me choose them all this time," Rowley said.

That afternoon Henny and the children went for a walk, with Sweep, of course. As they went along the esplanade, Henny looked again at the numbers of the six private houses. What a silly way to choose, she thought. She didn't tell the children.

Once they were on the beach, Henny let Sweep off his leash, and they soon found that his idea of fun was having a stick thrown for him to bring back. And how he could run! There wasn't much doubt of the whippet blood in his veins—he went like greased lightning. And when another dog—another Saltmouth stray by the look of it—came near Henny and the children, Sweep's hackles rose and he began to growl fiercely, as if to say, "This is *my* family. You get lost!" Which the other dog did.

Back at Ivy Cottage they all were hungry, especially Sweep. Henny now only fed him once a day, but she knew that the children slipped him bits of food under the table, and she had already caught both George and Mary offering him tidbits.

Sweep had not objected when George opened his mouth to inspect it.

"I'm no vet," said the dentist, "but I should think this was quite a young dog. He's got all forty-two teeth, in good condition, too."

"Forty-two?" said Mary. "That's one of your lottery numbers, Henny, isn't it? Now, we mustn't forget to watch the draw. Ten to eight. BBC 1."

At ten to eight sharp the seven Goods and Henny and Sweep (who only took notice when a dog appeared in a commercial on the TV, growling at it for daring to come into Ivy Cottage) sat watching the woman who would very soon be calling out the winning numbers. She was smiling, showing a lot of very white teeth.

"Nice set," said George critically.

He patted Sweep's black head.

"She's only got thirty-two," he said.

When all the razzmatazz was over and the machine was spinning, sending the colored balls—white, blue, pink, green, and yellow—dancing and jumping around, the starting button was pressed and the presenter said, "The flashing amber lights tell you when the balls have been selected." And then, "Here comes the first ball!"

It was a pink one. "Number twenty-one!"

Henny looked at her ticket.

"Well, at least we've got one right," she said.

"Here comes the second ball!" said the presenter. And as a green ball came down, "Number thirty-one!"

The children crowded around behind Henny to see the ticket.

"Look!" they said. "You've got that one right, too!"

The third ball was a white one. "Number six!"

"Yes!" cried the children. "You've got three, Henny!"

"You've won ten pounds," said Mary.

Then down came another white ball. "Number one!"

"Yes!" shouted the children.

"I can't believe it!" said Henny.

The fifth ball was a pink one. "Number twenty-six!"

The children yelled louder still.

"Don't tell me," said George. "She hasn't got that one, too?"

"Yes!" they shouted. "She's got all five so far!"

"What's the sixth one on the ticket?"

"Forty-two."

And then down the tube came a yellow ball, and spun, and stopped.

"And the sixth ball," said the presenter, "is number forty-two!" And all the Goods went crazy, whooping and cheering, while Henny's lucky dog barked and barked with excitement, showing all his forty-two teeth.

There was so much noise in the room that they

never heard the last number to be called, the bonus ball. Nor did they hear the voice of the announcer as she read out the six, now arranged in numerical order:

1   6   21   26   31   42

Henny had gotten them all!

"You've won, Henny!" the children shouted. "You've won the jackpot!"

"A share of it, anyway," said George. "There may be other people who got all six right, you know."

"We can find out," Mary said. "You can telephone and they'll tell you what the total jackpot is and how many people it is divided between. I've got the number somewhere. Here it is. Oh, George, you call, will you?"

George dialed the number and they all fell silent, listening.

"I understand," George said, "that you can tell me the total of the jackpot for this week's national lottery?"

And then:

"I see. And how many winners were there?"

And then:

"I see. Thank you. Good-bye."

"Well?" cried everyone. "Well?"

"Good thing you didn't tear up that ticket and throw it into the fire, Henny," said George. "The arithmetic is easy. The total jackpot is £10 million and there were ten correct answers. Henny, you have just won a million pounds."

"*We* have won a million pounds," said Henny. She went over to Mary and gave her a hug.

"You promised," she said. "Remember? It's £500,000 for each of us. Better than a poke in the eye with a blunt stick, as my mother used to say."

14

Remembering

Winning a great deal of money is a good thing for some people, and for others it is a bad thing.

Some may spend wisely and save wisely. Others may not save at all but instead spend wildly—on new houses, new cars, expensive clothes, foreign vacations, on any and every luxury that they never enjoyed before but now can afford (they think).

There were some of this second kind, no doubt, among the other nine winners of that week's jackpot, but for the Ivy Cottage winners there was never any question of frittering the money away.

George and Mary Good were comfortably off anyway, fortunate enough already to have most of the things they wanted in life, and when the claim had been made and the money paid, they invested it all, carefully, as a nest egg that would in due course see them through their old age.

They had no wish to change their lifestyle. George went to work in his dental office as usual, and Mary kept house, but with plenty of time now—thanks to Henny's helping hands—to pursue her French studies. Both George and Mary had tried their hardest to persuade Henny that it was rightly all *her* money, the whole million pounds, but she was not to be moved.

"You promised to take half," she said, "and that's what you're getting."

Henny herself had never had any money worth speaking of. She had never had a checkbook or a bank account, so she asked George's help in dealing with her £500,000.

He introduced her to his bank manager, and between them they fixed matters up so that she would never need to worry about money again.

She did spend some money, however. The very first check she wrote (the first she'd ever written in her life) was for quite a large sum as a gift to the Saltmouth Cottage Hospital.

And though the beach café was closed for the

winter, she found out the address of the owner, the man who had let her have £3 worth of ice cream for a penny, the whole of her worldly wealth. A delivery van arrived at his door with a case of whisky "From a well-wisher." Who had sent it, he never found out.

So the months went by at Ivy Cottage, while in the bedroom of the apartment Henny's money plant grew slowly but surely, as did the money in her new savings account.

That was really the only thing that worried Henny. Not only did she have this large amount of wealth, but it was sitting there getting larger. And I don't need it, she thought. I've got everything I want, here in my dear little room, with my dog, and my friends George and Mary, and their red-haired children of whom I have become so fond. What should I do with all these riches? What will happen to it all when I'm gone?

As usual, the voice of the late Mrs. Hickathrift sounded in her head at that moment.

"Where there's a will, there's a way," she heard her mother say. A will, thought Henny. "A will!" she said, and the next time she saw George, she asked him for the address of his lawyer.

"I want to make my will," she said.

Oh, dear, thought George. He looked at her critically. She looks pretty good, he thought, considering she must be nearly seventy-six by now—she's been with us almost a year. I must say, she's got a mouthful of really good teeth now, even if most of them aren't her own.

"Are you ill, Henny?" he asked.

"No, George, I'm fine," Henny said. "It's just that I've never made a will, so I think it would be wise."

"Of course. Good idea."

Henny never told him or anyone except her lawyer what that last will and testament of Henrietta Hickathrift contained. After a sum of money had been set aside for funeral expenses ("We've all got to die sometime!" Henny told the lawyer cheerfully), this was what the will said:

> I GIVE AND APPOINT all my estate
> of whatsoever kind and whereso-
> ever situate and everything over

which I have any disposing power by will unto Angela, Barney, Eleanor, Rosie, and Rowley Good, to be equally divided between them and distributed when each attains the age of eighteen years.

"Rowley, the youngest, is five now," she told the lawyer, "so that leaves him thirteen years to go. But with a bit of luck I might be around to see him old enough to get his share. I'll only be just coming up to my eighty-ninth birthday."

On her seventy-sixth birthday that summer Henny had a lovely party at Ivy Cottage. Mary made a beautiful birthday cake and on it put two little china figures she had found in a knickknack shop—a little old lady and a black dog. Among many other things to eat there were prawn and mayonnaise sandwiches, and the cookies were, of course, squashed flies.

After tea George went back to his office to finish off the day's work, and the children went out on the lawn to play croquet.

"No," said Mary firmly, "you are *not* going to

help with the dishes, Henny. It's your birthday. Think of it, a whole year since the children brought you to the door! Now go on, off you go. Why don't you take Sweep for a walk on the beach? It's a lovely evening."

So Henny fetched her cane and Sweep's leash, and they set off along the esplanade and down the steps to the beach.

The sea was very calm, and they walked along the water's edge, where a great many seagulls were standing about. This gave Sweep the chance to do some high-speed gull chasing—good fun for him since the birds waited till the last moment before flying up out of his reach.

They went a long way across the sands, and by the time they returned the incoming tide had narrowed the beach and the vacationers had all gone back up to Seaview and Balmoral and Greengables, and all the other bed-and-break-fasts and hotels in the town.

Henny paused, recalling what had happened exactly one year ago.

"I'd just set eyes on you for the first time," she said to Sweep, "and you were homeless, like me.

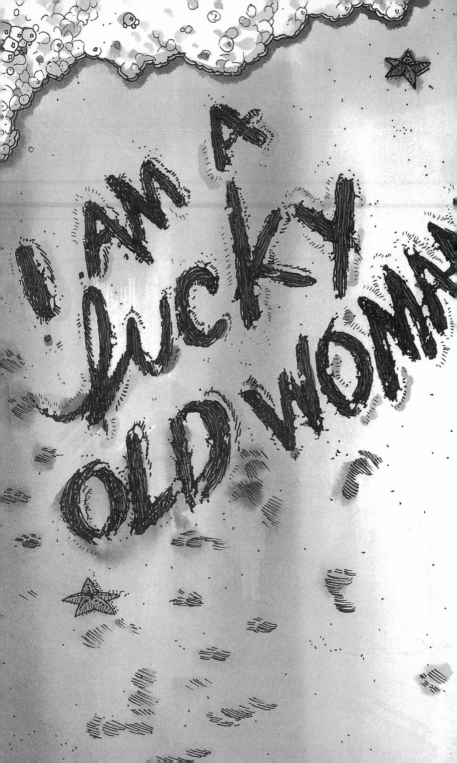

And then I wrote a message on the sand with my cane, like this."

When she had finished writing, she walked away, Sweep beside her, and climbed the long flight of steps that led to the esplanade high above. At the top she stopped to rest, leaning against the iron railing that flanked the road and looking down to the sands below. This time no one else was there to read what she had written on the sand in large letters. It was the same as the message of a year ago except for one different word:

I AM A LUCKY OLD WOMAN

it read.

Then Henrietta Hickathrift and her black dog, Sweep, turned and set off for home, while on the sands below the gentle waves washed out her happy words.

ABOUT THE AUTHOR

DICK KING-SMITH was born and raised in Gloucestershire, England. He served in the Grenadier Guards during World War II, then returned home to Gloucestershire to realize his life-long ambition of farming. After twenty years as a farmer, he turned to teaching and then to writing the children's books that have earned him many fans on both sides of the Atlantic. Inspiration for his writing comes from his farm and his animals.

Among his well-loved novels are *Babe: The Gallant Pig*, *Harry's Mad*, *Martin's Mice* (each an American Library Association Notable Book), *Ace: The Very Important Pig* (a *School Library Journal* Best Book of the Year), *The Toby Man*, *Paddy's Pot of Gold*, *Pretty Polly*, *The Invisible Dog*, *Three Terrible Trins*, and *Harriet's Hare* (*Parenting* Teading Magic Award). Additional honors and awards he has received are a *Boston Globe–Horn Book* Award (for *Babe: The Gallant Pig*) and the California Young Reader Medal (for *Harry's Mad*). In 1992 he was named Children's Author of the Year at the British Book Awards. In 1995 *Babe: The Gallant Pig* became a critically acclaimed major motion picture.